KU-337-426

LONDON'S
BURNING

LONDON'S BURNING

by Pauline Francis
and Alessandro Baldanzi

First published 2007
Evans Brothers Limited
2A Portman Mansions
Chiltern St
London W1U 6NR

British Library Cataloguing in Publication Data

Francis, Pauline
    London's burning. - (Skylarks)
    1. London (England) - Juvenile fiction 2. Children's
    stories
    I. Title
    823.9'14[J]

ISBN-13: 9780237533878 (hb)
ISBN-13: 9780237534059 (pb)

Printed in China by WKT Co. Ltd.

Series Editor: Louise John
Design: Robert Walster
Production: Jenny Mulvanny

Contents

Chapter One

A very long time ago – in 1666 – a boy called John had just gone to bed.

He slept in a little attic in the roof of a tall wooden house.

"I can't go to sleep," said John. "It's too dark up here! Can I have a candle, *please*, Mother?"

"No!" said his mother. "Candles can start fires. But I'll let Kitty sleep with you."

Kitty was John's ginger cat. She ran up the ladder and jumped onto John's bed. John's house was in Crooked Lane, not far from the River Thames in London. And his friend Elizabeth lived in the house opposite. The street was so narrow that the attic window of Elizabeth's house almost touched John's.

John opened his little window. "Elizabeth!" he called out. "I've got Kitty with me tonight."

Elizabeth leaned out of her window. She stretched across the narrow street to John's window and stroked Kitty.

"I can see London Bridge from here!" boasted John.

"I can see St Paul's Cathedral from here!" boasted Elizabeth.

"I'm having a candle in my room tonight!" said John.

"You're too young!" laughed Elizabeth.

"No, I'm not!" said John. "You wait and see."

Later, when his mother and father had fallen asleep by the fire, John crept downstairs. He took their candle and tiptoed back up the ladder to his bedroom. Then he put the candle on his windowsill.

Elizabeth came to her window again. They made shadow puppets with their fingers against the wall and talked and laughed together until they were sleepy.

"Goodnight, John," said Elizabeth,

closing her window.

"Goodnight, Elizabeth," said John, getting into bed.

John left his window open because he wanted to watch his candle in the breeze. And at last, the flickering candlelight sent him to sleep.

Chapter Two

Not far away, in Pudding Lane, lived a
baker. His bread was so delicious that
he had been asked especially to make it
for the king. The baker was going to

bed early. He had to get up at four o'clock in the morning to start baking the bread.

"Put out the fire before you go to sleep," he told the baker boy. "Make sure you pour on plenty of water. And don't forget. There's straw all over the floor here."

But the baker boy was tired, too, because he'd worked hard all day. He yawned, closed his eyes and fell immediately asleep. And, as he slept, a spark jumped from the fire onto the straw, where it caught light.

John woke up in the middle of the night. How hot it was! He pushed Kitty away, but he was still too hot. He went to the window to breathe in some fresh air. But, strangely, even the air outside was hot. John peered out.

"That's funny," thought John. "I can't see London Bridge. And I can't see the River Thames. Why is the sky so black tonight?"

As John watched, red and yellow flames rose into the sky near London Bridge. Suddenly, the night was as light as day. John was scared. The flames crackled dangerously and he could smell burning.

John suddenly remembered the candle he had taken from his parents.

"Oh no!" whispered John. "My candle

isn't there! It must have fallen over into the street. I've set London on fire! What am I going to do?"

John ran down the ladder and went to wake his mother and father.

"Fire! Fire!" he shouted. "Help! Help!"

Chapter Three

"John, calm down! What on earth is wrong?" asked John's mother and father, anxiously.

John told his mother and father about the flames and the smoke. They looked through the window into the street. All

the houses in Crooked Lane were in darkness. Everybody was in bed.

"Go back to sleep, John," they said. "You've been dreaming."

John held Kitty tightly and went back to bed. He was so tired that he fell asleep straight away.

Early the next morning, the ringing of the church bells woke John. The sky was still dark. "That's strange," thought John. "I know it's Sunday, but it's still too early to go to church. What's happening?"

John coughed. Smoke! It stung his eyes and throat. He looked through the window. The fire hadn't been a dream after all, and it had almost reached London Bridge! Then he heard his father's voice.

"John," he called, "get dressed!
Quickly! You were right. London *is*
burning! We have to leave NOW!"

John put on his clothes and ran
downstairs. His mother opened the door
onto the street. The thatched roof of a

nearby house was already on fire. Red
flames were licking the upstairs window.

People were running along the street.
Some shouted, "Fire! Fire!" Others
shouted, "Pour on water!"

The flames hissed. And they were

coming towards John's house! Kitty didn't like the smoke or the noise. She hid under the table.

John's heart pounded in his chest. "It's all my fault!" he thought.

"The wind is blowing the flames towards us," John's mother shouted. "We can't get out through the door now. Quickly! Up the ladder! We'll have to escape across the rooftops."

Chapter Four

John's mother quickly wrapped some
clothes in a blanket and put some bread
and cheese into a basket. She climbed
the ladder first with Kitty. John and his
father followed her. John's mother
squeezed through the little attic window
onto the roof.

Then she held out her hand to John.

"Come on!" she said. "We must escape
across the roof before it catches fire.
Quickly, before it's too late."

"I can't," cried John. "I'll fall."

The smoke became thicker. John
couldn't see Elizabeth's house at all. And
he could only just see his mother's hand.

Downstairs, the flames were already coming through the front door. The table and chairs were burning. The house grew hotter and hotter.

"Hurry!" said John's father from behind.

But John froze on the spot. He was too scared to move. Kitty came and licked John's face. Then she jumped through the window and waited for him.

"Kitty wants you to follow her, John," said his mother. "Come on, you can do it. You'll be safe with her."

John had never been so frightened in his life but he wriggled through the window. Then he helped his father to climb through. Holding his father's hand, John followed Kitty carefully through the smoke. They walked across the rooftops, until they were a long way away from the fire. When they eventually looked back, they couldn't see their house. It was hidden by a thick cloud of black smoke.

"We're safe now," said John's father. "Let's climb down to the street again."

When they were in the street, John buried his face in Kitty's fur. "Thank you so much for saving me," he whispered.

Chapter Five

After reaching the ground, John and his mother and father set off for the fields outside London. But the streets were full of people. Everybody was pushing and pulling and children were crying.

"I don't like it here," said John.

As they walked, they heard the hissing flames coming closer and closer. Smoke filled the street. John's mother picked up Kitty and put her in the basket.

"Who's going to put out the fire?" asked John.

"The king has come to help us," said his father. "His men are pulling down the houses around the fire, so that it

can't spread any further."

"I wish I could see the king," said John.

Suddenly, a shower of sparks fell from the roof above them. Everybody around

was screaming "Fire! Help!"

John panicked and accidentally let go
of his father's hand. When he looked up
again, he couldn't see his father at all.

"Father!" shouted John.

But John's father couldn't get back to him because there were too many people. At first, John didn't know what to do. Then he hid in a doorway and waited for somebody to find him.

"Boy!" John looked up. The voice came from a man on a white horse. He was wearing fine clothes and a hat with a long feather in it. He was carrying a stick to beat out the flames.

"Are you lost?" asked the man.

John nodded. "I was with my mother and father," he said. "We were on our way to the fields outside London. But I don't know how to get there."

"Jump up behind me," said the man. "I'll take you."

When they reached the fields, John was surprised to see so many people and

even more surprised when all of them stood up and cheered as the horse went past them.

At last they found John's father. He had taken John's mother safely to the fields. Now he was on his way back to look for John. To John's surprise, his father bowed. "Thank you for saving my son, Your Majesty," he said.

John gasped. "But how can you be the king?" he asked. "Your clothes are far too dirty."

The king laughed. "Putting out fires is dirty work," he said. "And, believe me, it is harder work than being a king."

He turned his horse around. "Now I must

go back to fighting the fire," he said. He took off his hat, waved it in the air and rode back towards London.

John sat down and told his mother about his exciting adventure. She laughed and cried at the same time.

33

Then she pointed to the hill at the top of the field.

"Elizabeth is waiting for you," she said.

John ran to the top of the hill and hugged Elizabeth.

"I'm so glad you're safe," cried John.

John and Elizabeth looked at each other and laughed because they were both dirty from top to toe. Then they sat down to watch the fire. The flames grew higher and hotter. And the people looked like ants as they scurried towards

the river. They were trying to escape
London by boat.

"I reckon three hundred houses have
burned already," John's father said.
"But London Bridge has been saved."

John's heart was beating very fast.
"It's all my fault," he thought again.

Chapter Six

On Monday, the wind was stronger. It blew the flames faster and faster across the city. More and more houses burned. Some of the king's men blew up houses with gunpowder to stop the fire spreading to the Tower of London. John could hear all the noise from the top of the hill.

On Tuesday, another loud noise woke John up. It was like the sound of a gun. Everybody ran from their tents to see what was happening.

"The fire has reached St. Paul's Cathedral," said John's father. "The stones are so hot that they're shooting into the air. Look!"

John's father sat him on his shoulders.
It was true. St. Paul's Cathedral was in
flames. The metal on its roof was
melting and running along the street
like a red river.

"This is the worst day of all," said John's father. His face was sad. "London will never be the same again."

John couldn't bear it any longer. He began to cry.

"Don't worry," said John's mother. "We're safe here and that's what matters. People are more important than buildings."

"But it's all my fault!" cried John. "I took your candle upstairs when you were asleep. I set London on fire!"

His mother smiled. "No, you didn't. I took the candle away when you were asleep," she said. "This fire started in the baker's shop in Pudding Lane." She gave him a big hug. "It wasn't your fault, John."

John was delighted and relieved at the

same time. "It wasn't my fault! It wasn't my fault!" he sang. He caught hold of Elizabeth and they danced round and round, with Kitty chasing after them.

Chapter Seven

On Wednesday, the wind stopped blowing. One by one, the fires went out. The sky was blue again and John and his family could see London clearly.

But some of the city looked very different. There were no houses, no shops and no churches. There were only piles of burned wood in every direction they looked.

The next day, it was finally safe for John and his father to walk back into London. At last, they came to Crooked Lane. All the houses had been burned

there, too. A pile of wood ash glowed red where John's house had been.

"Look, Father," whispered John, sadly.

"Yes, John, but we need to remember that we are lucky to be alive," replied his father. John and his father stood and looked at what was left of Crooked Lane. They were sad that their house had been burned, but happy that nobody in Crooked Lane had died in the fire.

"And all the rats have run away," said John's father, with a smile.

"What will happen to us, now?" asked John.

"King Charles is a kind king," said John's father. "He will look after us all just like he looked after you when you were lost in the fire."

He put his arm around John's shoulders. "Don't worry, London will be beautiful again one day, John, you'll see."

And it is, isn't it?

If you enjoyed this story, why not read another *Skylarks* book?

Hurricane Season

by David Orme and Doreen Lang

Grace and her family had come to Florida on holiday to visit Grandma and Grandpa. Mum and Dad were staying in a hotel on Palm Beach but Grace wanted to stay in Grandma and Grandpa's trailer. She hadn't been there long when the weather started to change. There was going to be a hurricane and it was going to be a big one!

Detective Derek
by Karen Wallace and Beccy Blake

Derek was no ordinary cat. He was
a cat with a difference.

If dogs could be in the police force,
why not cats? So, when all the other
cats were out chasing mice, Detective
Derek and his partner Sergeant Norman
were out on top secret police business –
they were on a mission to catch the
Mouse and the Boxer, the sneakiest
crooks in town…

Skylarks titles include:

Awkward Annie
by Julia Williams and Tim Archbold
HB 9780237533847
PB 9780237534028

Sleeping Beauty
by Louise John and Natascia Ugliano
HB 9780237533861
PB 9780237534042

Detective Derek
by Karen Wallace and Beccy Blake
HB 9780237533885
PB 9780237534066

Hurricane Season
by David Orme and Doreen Lang
HB 9780237533892
PB 9780237534073

Spiggy Red
by Penny Dolan and Cinzia Battistel
HB 9780237533854
PB 9780237534035

London's Burning
by Pauline Francis and Alessandro Baldanzi
HB 9780237533878
PB 9780237534059